THAT

GIRL

LINDA OATMAN HIGH

SADDLEBACK
EDUCATIONAL PUBLISHING

GRAVEL ROAD

SADDLEBACK
EDUCATIONAL PUBLISHING
www.sdlback.com

Copyright ©2016 by Saddleback Educational Publishing
All rights reserved. No part of this book may be reproduced in any form or by any means, electronic
or mechanical, including photocopying, recording, scanning, or by any information storage and
retrieval system, without the written permission of the publisher. SADDLEBACK EDUCATIONAL
PUBLISHING and any associated logos are trademarks and/or registered trademarks of Saddleback
Educational Publishing.

ISBN-13: 978-1-68021-060-6
ISBN-10: 1-68021-060-2
eBook: 978-1-63078-376-1

Printed in Guangzhou, China
NOR/1015/CA21501470

20 19 18 17 16   1 2 3 4 5

Gravel Road

VERSE

#ClickPicQuick

Fine.
        I was taking
                a selfie
                        when I died.

No lie.
My brain
was fried.

                Distracted.
                Impacted.

                        (And no,
                        as a matter
                                of fact,
                        I was not
                        on crack!)

Wacked, but
accidents
happen.

                    True that.

                              (That's why
                                   they call
                                       them
                              "accidents.")

Hold the phone.
                    Click. Pic. Sick!
Post it
quick!

I didn't know
that stupid road
was so
slick …

#PlusThatSquirrel

Plus
there
was
that
squirrel.*

It
ran
right
into
my
path.

Just
seconds
before

* #TheForest

3

the
crash.

poor
little
furry
squirrel
+
selfie
girl
=

SWERVE

#AllAboutMe

It was like
Instagram.

BAM!

Jamming,
slamming
with the band
Why So Bitter?

Planning
to go

on Twitter.

Also

my Facebook post.

(Social media is most crucial when you're 17 and
you need to be social and/or emotional.)

Believe me,
  composing
    your post
      while driving
        is not that
          unusual.

I'll tweet about how

@THATSELFIEGIRL

> sweet it is to rock this new blue hand-
> knitted retro sweater, even better in
> such amazing springtime weather!

And my skirt is
vintage
brown leather.

My hair is braided
and beaded
with real
feathers!

So?

You think that I—Macy Elaine Rain—
is—was—
crazy-vain?

Whatever.

#SoNotCool

It is so
not cool
to be
aiming
the phone
at your
great
zit-free
face
on a good
no-grease
hair day
one minute,

and then
dead
the next.

#BloodAndGlass

I was covered in blood
and smashed-up fragments
of glass.

Shards like
diamonds shimmered—

glimmered—

on my skin,
which was actually
kind of pretty,

                                except not,

considering
the circumstances.

#WayLongHome

The song
playing
was "Way Long Home."

My Facebook post came straight from Twitter.

MACY ELAINE RAIN   *1 min ago*   **Comment**   **Like**

> *I love Why So Bitter?*
> *Digging song*
> *Way Long Home!* ☺

That post,
along with my picture,
was my very last
tweet.

#ItAllHappenedSoFast

My post
loaded online

at 9:45,

the same time
as the first

911

call
was recorded.

The lights
and sirens
flared
and blared

at 9:49.

I was pronounced
dead

at 10:10 a.m.

(And yes,
we know time
in the afterlife.

Heaven has schedules
too.)

#TheSongGoesOn

The song
"Way Long
Home"
just kept on
playing,
all 3 minutes
28
seconds
of it,
after
I was
already dead.

The song played.
Cops prayed.

An ambulance
man made
the sign of the cross.

A firefighter sat in the moss, gnawing on
her perfectly painted red nails.

Major fail.
I'd already
bailed.

#DeadDeadDeadDeadDeadDead

Nomorebreath   Nomoreheart

Just   Dead

#FarAway

Gasoline sprayed
from my
crashed-up,
smashed-up,
bashed-up
grandmother-tan
Impala.

(The car used to
belong to Grandma,
and then
she gave it
to me.)

I could see
Grandma's face
from above,
lined with years

of love,
wearing her
fancy satin
gloves.
She was at
a formal
breakfast
with her
best friend,
Evelyn,
at a place
called
A Taste
of Heaven.

A painting fell
right beside
their
table.

"There's an old
wives' tale," Grandma says to Evelyn.

"When a picture
falls
from a wall,
it means someone
you love
has just
gone."

"Oh, my,"
says Evelyn.
"I hope
that's wrong."

#25PeopleLikeThis

Friends kept
giving thumbs-up
on my Facebook post.

SLEDGE *at 9:46 am* **Reply** **Like**
Beautiful girl!

said my best friend,
Sledge.

BENNETT *at 9:47 am* **Reply** **Like**
Uber-hot!

posted some dude   I don't know.

BEX *at 9:47 am* **Reply** **Like**

I like how your nose piercing sparkles in the sunlight!

OTTO *at 9:48 am* **Reply** **Like**

Nice smile!

CARMA *at 9:49 am* **Reply** **Like**

Beautiful day to be alive!

There were 25 likes
before anybody
knew
that I'd
died.

#WalmartSpecial

The Walmart truck
I hit head-on
was only slightly
smashed. Bashed
a little bit in the front.

The driver was fine,
but he just
kept screaming,
eyes wild.

        "It's a child!"

            Dude. Chill out.
        Chillax. You'll have
          a heart attack.
        And by the way,

I am—was—
not a little kid.
Relax a bit!
I still live.

#FlashbackGoodbye

You know   how they say   your entire life
flashes before your eyes   as you die?   Well,
            that's not   exactly right.

What flashes   before your eyes   is actually
                  the last
                  goodbye.

#MomAndGoodbye

Mom at the back door
this morning, acting corny.

She waved goodbye.
Made a peace sign.
And she was dancing
some weird 1980's move.

"I'm in the groove!" Mom said.

"Were you drinking wine?"
I asked, laughing.
"You're so wacked."

We cracked up.

Mom blew me a kiss
as I got in my car
and started it.

"Don't text while
you drive!" she called.
"It can wait. And don't
forget, we have a date.
Movie night."

"All right, all right," I said.
I shook my head.

And that's the
last thing
I said
to my mom
before I was
dead.

I'd
not
yet
confessed
the
secret
to
my
parents.
I
had
a
dream
the
night
before
the
accident.
In
the
dream

I
heard
the
words
"You
need
to
tell
the
police."

#SucksToBeMe

The sun shone.
The sky glowed blue.

Happy birds chirped in trees.
There was an autumn breeze.
Plus the falling leaves.

But geez,
my hair was
a freakin'
crappy tangle.

I was mangled.
Blood blended
into my sweater.
Seeping red

wet
my face.

Yes, it
definitely
sucked
to
be
me.

And here's
the best
—yet worst—
part of
this
entire
mess.

I was headed
to the
police station
to confess.

Yes,
I'd finally decided
it was best
to tell them
what I knew
—what I
still know—
about
Ryan Dunew.

He has
this Big Plan
to shoot up
the school.

So.
Not.
Cool.

#ThatSelfieGirl

"Oh," said
people who did
not know
me.

"That Selfie Girl,
Macy Rain?
She was always
posting pics
of herself!
Like, 24/7!
Wonder if she's
doing that
up there
in
Heaven?"

Gossip
and drama.
Cattiness and
brattiness.

Too.
Much.
Drama.

They
Don't
Know
Me.

Truth is,
I am half-
happy
to get away
from all
the crappy
drama
of Green Line High.

What they
don't know
is that I was on my
way to the
police station
to save
their lives.

And I am more …
much,
much,
so much
more …

than just
              That
                   Selfie
                       Girl.

#TheySay

They say
maybe
I was dating
Ryan Dunew.

This is *so*
not true!

We did not
hook up!
We were just
discussing

his **depression**
and his **confession**

about what he
planned to do
at school.

They say
my face
looked fat
in that
last selfie.
And that
maybe I
was having
a baby!
With Ryan Dunew!

                                                    So
                                                   Not
                                                  True!

They say
maybe
Macy Rain
was on drugs.
That maybe
Macy was
a meth head

or on crack
when she
crashed.

So
Not
True!

They say
Macy Rain
drank too much
rum at that party
one time
last summer.
And wasn't it
a bummer
that Macy Rain
didn't just
sign up for
AA or something
so she wouldn't
be a drunk,

like,
all the rest
of her
life.

I was
not a drunk.
I drank that rum
because somebody
mixed it
into my Pepsi.

> "I heard that
> maybe Macy Rain
> had narcolepsy,
> or epilepsy,
> and had a seizure
> that day,"
> they say.

> Oh, please!
> Just shut up!

I did not have
a sleeping disease
or a seizure disease
or *any*
disease!
Except maybe
I just cared
too much.
I was too
sensitive.

The lesson
for you

(or for
they who say)

is that
next time
you gossip
about somebody
dead or
about pregnancy
or hooking up

or drugs
or rum
or disease
or who dated who …

Just remember—
PLEASE!—
that in Heaven

we can
hear
you.

#ALesson

I'm used
as a lesson   in Driver's Ed.
All about
how you could be   **dead**
if you text
while driving.

I am the poster child
for death   **by text**.

I am plotting
how to change
this
image.

#DeadPeopleHaveFeelingsToo

This
Much
Is
True.
Dead
People
Have
Feelings
Too.

We
Are
Still
Human.

#TheCar

The crashed
          Impala
               went to the
                    junkyard.

          Dumped, crippled

with other
crashed-up
cars.

It looks so
sad, like
a crumpled tissue
that somebody
cried into.

That old
tan
car

took me
nice and far
in my life.
Like that time
Sledge and I
drove all
the way
to the beach.

I don't want that
car to just be
a hunk of junk.

So what I do
is decide to
add some light.

I grab a chunk
of star,
and I reach down
to my car,
inside
the glass and steel.

I feel the
darkness inside
that car, and so
I throw
in a chunk
of star.

The headlights
come on,
light in the night,
shining bright.

I like
being
Queen of Light.

#Pieces

Sledge walks
along the side
of the road
where I crashed.

His eyes
are on the ground,
in the grass,
where the last
pieces of me
and my car
rest.

Sledge bends down.
He picks up a hunk
of shattered glass

from the windshield.
Puts it in his pocket.

He picks up a chunk
of red taillight and
a piece of twisty metal.

"I'm going to make
an angel from this,
Macy," Sledge says.
"It'll hang on
our Christmas tree.
Just to remind me
of you. Maybe I'll
make one for your
parents too.
Use something broken
to make something whole."

Sledge was always
so cool.
He always knew

LINDA OATMAN HIGH

how to take
a wreck
and make
something beautiful
out of it.

Ryan
Dunew
Made
A
Wooden
Cross.
He
Painted
My
Name
Across
It.

MACY

ELAINE

RAIN

47

He
Planted
It

(REST IN PEACE)

In
The
Grass
Next
To
Where
I
Crashed.

"See
you
soon,"
he
whispers.

#IHateWhenThatHappens

So they postponed
the prom.

It was going to be
the bomb.

A *Great Gatsby* theme,
with antique
luggage trunks
stuffed with fluffy boas
and 1920's hats
and the kind of mask
you hold on a stick.

A jazz band
with a stand-up

bass player
and a chocolate fountain
for dipping pretzels
and old black-and-white
photos
of people's
dead relatives.

I had
a flapper dress
with fringe.
My date
was Sledge,
who's been
my best friend
since second grade.

Sledge had a zoot suit
and shiny wing-tip shoes.

*I ruined
everything.*

#IAmStillMacy

Mom curled,
hurling
on the
kitchen floor.

She hit
the yellow
tile
with her fists.

(Mom! Mellow!
Get some rest.
Take some breaths.)

Dad had
to get sedatives.

Mom refused meds.
She just kept
saying my name.

"Macy. Macy. Macy
MACY ELAINE RAIN!
Where are you?
Where did you go?
Come home!
MACY, COME HOME!"

I wish
they could know
I'm still at home.
Just not
with my skin.
Or my blood.
Or my bones.
Or my voice.
Or my face.
Or my brain.

Not my choice,
but …

I am still Macy.

#ItHurts

To see them cry.
To know
it's because
I
died.

There's nowhere
to
hide.

#Grandma

Grandma is
not wearing her
usual dress.
She's a mess.
No lipstick
or big sparkly
gem earrings.

She trembles.
Shakes. Bakes
a lemon cake
to get her
mind off
her sweet
little
Macy Rain.

It doesn't work.
The cake just
makes
it worse
because it was
my favorite.

"Oh, if only
I didn't give her
that car!" Grandma
says
out loud
to her kitchen
walls.
"If only she couldn't
drive, she'd still be
alive!"

Oh, Grandma,
it was my time.
You are still
alive.

So just try,
please,
just try
to smile.

It's only
a short while
until we are
together
again.

You see,
in Heaven
we know
who will
come
next.

#DustIsJustDeadPeople

When
You
Dust,
You
Are
Just
Swiping,
Wiping,
Brushing
Away
The
Fine
Remains
Of
Those
Who   no   longer   remain.

#MyBigDay

I won't get
to have
a wedding.

So this
is
my
big day.

Funeral day.
Some kids
wear their
prom clothes.

So I have
a *Great Gatsby*

kind of vibe
for my big day.

There are lots
of photos of me.

But thankfully
not the famous selfie.

The preacher
blabs about
Heaven and faith,
and everybody sings
"Amazing Grace."

Pink and blue
helium balloons
fly,
released into
the sky
outside.

Some people
look high.

And here's
something
especially
weird:

There's
Ryan Dunew
acting all blue.
As if
he does not
have Big Plans

and a room
full
of guns.

#DaddysLittleGirl

On his way
to work,
Dad takes a
short detour
to the cemetery
where my body
is buried.

He gets out,
places flowers
on the stone
engraved with
my
name
and two dates.

"Macy," Dad says
to the stone.
"I wish I could
call you on the
phone.
Just to hear your
voice
one more time
would be
so fine.
I remember the
day you were
born,
just like
yesterday.
My pretty little
baby girl.
My princess.
I miss you so
much, sweetheart."

Dad cries for a while.
Collapses weeping.
He's usually good
at keeping
his feelings
inside.
But this …
this … this
he can't hide.
I try to
open a flower petal
a little bit more.
Right before his
eyes.
So that Dad
might know
that I am
still alive.

His princess
still exists.

#RyanDunew

Ryan Dunew,
in his room,
and he's so full
of sadness and
frustration and
anger and depression
and confusion.

He is hopeless.
He can't cope.
Ryan is at the
end of his rope.

Ryan Dunew
takes his medication.

"Why doesn't it work?"
he says out loud.
"It never works.
I'm so tired of feeling
like a jerk. Maybe I
should just end it
now."

Ryan gets
on his bed,
and he cries.
"I miss you, Macy,"
he says.
"You were the only
one I could talk to
out of the whole
freakin' school.
I don't even know
what to do.
So, yeah,
I'll definitely
see you soon."

Hang in there,
Ryan. Don't shoot
up the school.
Don't commit suicide.
Everything bad
eventually gets
better. Or at least
good enough.
Be tough.
Be strong.
Listen to your
songs.
Play your guitar.
Look outside,
up at the stars,
Ryan.
That's where I
am.
I am listening.
You can still
talk to me.

Ryan stops weeping.
Sits up in his bed.
He presses his head
to the window,
and I see his eyes.
They are wet with tears.

"Are you still here?"
he says.

He looks up,
staring at the stars.

I'm here.
I'm not as far
as you think.
I'm shining
for you,
Ryan Dunew.

#Sledge

Sledge's real name
is Ray. We changed
his name to Sledge
in second grade
because he pounded
on things.
Like a hammer.

Sledge is hyper.
ADHD.
He's creative
and quirky.
A piece of work.

Sledge wears
these

1950's glasses,
and he has a
punk haircut:
green-dyed spikes.

We were best friends
for so long
that being without him
now
feels wrong.

He is writing
a song for me.
The title is
"Macy Rain: Can't Explain."

Sledge has the
most amazing brain.
Some people think
he's insane.
He dances in rain.
He likes to

raise Cain.
And sometimes
he is just
a royal pain.

But for some reason
none of this
stuff
bothers me.

Sledge and I
are bonded
tight. It's like
our hearts
are superglued
together, and
nobody
can separate
them.

Not even death.
Every breath

for Sledge
still includes
me.

And I'm flying.
I'm in the sky
over Sledge's
spiky green head.

I feel his breath.
I hear his song.
His heart beats
inside of me,
and my heart beats
inside of him.

He is eating a
Slim Jim.

"Remember how
you hated beef jerky?"
Sledge says to me out loud.

"Well, Macy, now
you will never know
what you missed.
I'm kind of pissed
about that.
Does Heaven include
beef jerky?"

OMG. LOL.

*I think Hell
includes beef
jerky, I say
back to him.*

Sledge chows
down on that
Slim Jim,
and
on a whim
he holds it up
to the sky.

"Here," he says.
"Just try!"

I sigh,
and my breath
is a breeze
on Sledge's face
as I race away
to the place
I must go
next.

#DeadIsHardToExplain

Dead is hard to explain.
It's almost
like a movie
playing inside
your brain.   *Except not.*

You see things.
You know things.
You hear things.
You smell things.

I am still Macy Elaine Rain.

Oh snap.
It's just
so hard
to explain.

#TheDisneyRideToTheAfterlife

It takes
8 days—
8 Earth days—
to arrive.

Before that
you are flying
in the sky.

It's almost
like a Disney ride
that requires
no waiting
in line
or buying
of tickets.

Death is
weight free,
hate free,
pain free,
vain free.

It's so
relaxing,
chillaxing,
like floating
on your back
in the quietest
swimming pool
ever to exist.

Except
there's no water.

There is only color.

You are alone,
totally alone,

except that you
feel the love
of about a zillion
million
trillion others.
It's like a
mother's love.
Unconditional.

Trust me on this. It friggin' rocks.

It's true!
If only
you knew.

If you had
half a clue.

You wouldn't be
all whiny
about
dead people.

#WhatYouKnow

You think about stuff. You feel love.

You know there's grief,
and you know it's deep.

But you also know
there's not really a real reason to weep.

Because you know
we will all go
to the
same place.

Eventually.

It just takes patience.

#TheKidsOnTheList

Who I think
about most
is Ryan Dunew.

And I have no clue
how to get *that* news

through

to the people
in charge.

It is almost the end of May,
and that is the day
when
Ryan will go to

Green Line High,
in Green Line, Ohio.

And he has no intent
to walk the green mile.

He will
kill himself
right after

he gets rid
of all those kids.
The kids
on his list.

And if Ryan's designs
go
without a hitch,

life will
be a total bitch
for those left behind.

#StreetsOfGold

Streets of gold?
Dude. It's true,
but it's a gold
like you've
never known.
There are fountains
too.
Even a chocolate
fountain
high as a
mountain.

I wonder
if there
is prom
here too.

#PuffyLove

So there
are just
all these
fluffy
souls,
and you just
kind of know.

Love,
      puffed up
            like a marshmallow
                  in the sun.

#MySectionOfHeaven

Heaven is kind of
like New York City,
except beautiful,
with sections.

There's the
Died from Cancer
section and the
Suicide section
and the Passed Away
from Old Age
section.

There's a Crib Death section
and an
Under 11 Years

section and a
Killed by Knives
section. There's a
Killed by Guns
section.

And a Died by Jumping
section.

And OMG,
there's even an
Ebola section.

None of them are
mine.

So I'm looking
for a Died by Car Accident
sign,
and all
of a sudden
there's a tour guide.

#NoSecrets

"May I help you,
darlin'?"
he asks
in a Southern
accent.

His nametag
says Samuel.

He has red hair
and a soul patch
on his chin.

"Um, yes. Please.
You can help me.
My name
is Macy Rain,

and I died
on May 8th.
Green Line, Ohio,
Highway 9."

Samuel lights up.

"Well, my stars!"
he says. "I know
who you are!
That Selfie Girl!"

Oh, geez.

Even in Heaven
there are
no secrets.

#DiedByTexting

"You,
Miss Macy,
are in
the
Died
by Texting
section,"
Samuel says.

"But, but …
um,
it wasn't
texting. I wasn't
texting! I was *tweeting*
and *posting*."

"Child," Samuel says
with a kind
smile. "It's all
the same here.
We don't have time
to get that specific."

It's Heaven!
Don't they have,
like, all eternity?

#LecturesInHeaven

"It happened
with a cell phone,
with you
pushing buttons
on that
phone,"
Samuel says.

"And not paying
attention to anything
else around you.

All because
you wanted
a picture
of your face,

to show off to
the human race
how pretty
you were!

I swear,
everybody in
America
is just click-click-
clicking
pictures
of their own
faces!"

"Well, it's not
exactly pushing
buttons,"
I try
to explain.
"It's a smartphone,
you see,
so you just kind

of touch
the screen."

"I know
about phones,
girlfriend. How
about a little
respect? You
still belong
in the
Died by Texting
section."

Okay, okay,
I'm thinking.

I didn't know
there were lectures
in Heaven too.

Dude.

#AfterlifeFAQs

"I have a million questions
about Heaven," I say
to Samuel. "Like, for example,
if a baby dies, is that baby
still a baby here?"

Samuel produces a brochure.
The title is *Afterlife FAQs:*
Frequently
Asked Questions
About Heaven.

Q: What is there to do in Heaven?

A: Anything you want to do! It's all free. It's
all easy. And it's always 70 degrees and breezy!

Q: Do we need to sleep? Do we need to eat?

A: We don't need to eat or to sleep, but most souls prefer to do both. Because eating and sleeping bring back fond memories of your best times on Earth. It's worth a try!

Q: Will we cry here? Is it true that there is no more pain or tears in Heaven?

A: Yes! Pain has gone away. And the only tears you will find here are in the saltwater pools located in the town square. Those tears are collected from years and years of crying done on Earth.

Q: Will I get to meet God?

A: God is very popular, as you might imagine. If you wish to meet God, please add your name to the God List. And please, be patient. Your turn will come.

Q: Do we really get a new body here? Do we

look like we looked on Earth? Are we the same age and in the same shape as when we passed on?

A: You are the same age in Heaven as you were when you died. You may stay that age, if you wish. Or you may choose to cruise back and forth between 0 and 100 years. Everyone is free of disease here. No more illness. No more aches and pains.

Q: Is there Facebook here? How about computers?

A: We have Soulbook. And computers for your use are located in the fresh juice area of Heaven.

Q: If I smoked on Earth, will I smoke here too?

A: Dude! Get a clue. No smoking.

Q: If I was not smart on Earth, will I not be smart here too?

A: Duh. That's the lamest question ever!

Q: What if I was smokin' hot down there?

A: Nobody really cares. We are not all about the outsides here in the afterlife.

Q: If I died in a horrible accident, will I still look all bloody in Heaven?

A: Of course not. Who wants to look at a bloody soul for all eternity? Gross!

Q: Is there love in Heaven?

A: Yes! Celestial romance is very popular here. After all, every relationship will be stress free.

Q: Is there marriage here? How about giving birth?

A: There can be marriage. Heaven is the perfect setting for a wedding! No giving birth. That is only done on Earth.

Q: Will I live with the same family I had on Earth?

A: We are one big happy family here. Just think of it like a 1960's hippie commune.

Q: Will I be able to see my Earth family? Like, watch what they are doing?

A: What are you, a creeper? A peeper? No stalking the people below. They will be joining you in the blink of an eye. Just try to forget about them for a while. And for God's sake, smile. After all, you are in Heaven!

Q: Why do we have both wings *and* arms?

A: Just another one of Heaven's many charms. We work hard to ensure your comfort.

Q: Is there PMS in Heaven?

A: Yes. Permanent Massive Silliness. Period.

Q: Will we stay forever in the section of Heaven we are assigned when we arrive?

A: Not necessarily. You may speak to your section supervisors for the rules about moving.

Q: What if someone annoys me, and I can't get away from them?

A: This is Heaven! There are lots of places to escape. Annoyance is to be avoided if at all possible.

Q: If I was naked when I passed away, will I be naked here?

A: It would be rude to be nude in Heaven. Nobody wants to see your Earth privates in a public afterlife.

Q: Do we need to take baths and showers here?

A: No need to bathe. Body odor has faded away.

Q: If I was gay on Earth, will I be gay here?

A: That is your choice. We rejoice in making all souls comfortable. In Heaven there is never any judgment.

Q: Is there sex in Heaven?

A: That is decided on an individual basis. Speak to Jesus at your convenience. He will take your personal details into consideration.

Q: Are there pets in Heaven?

A: Yes. Where do you think all those dead cats and dogs have gone?

Q: Will I sleep in a bed in Heaven?

A: If you wish. Or you might enjoy trying our Sleep-in-the-Clouds option. We offer cloud adoption for your convenience.

Q: Are there toilets in Heaven?

A: Of course not. No need for number 1 or number 2, or to make a big to do about cleaning toilets. Besides, who wants that odor in Heaven? If we had that smell, it would be more like Hell.

Q: Do the babies of Heaven wear diapers?

A: No. See above.

Q: Is talking allowed?

A: Yes. Some people love to yak, and others prefer to just kick back and relax.

Q: So our bodies will *never* grow old?

A: No. Also, there are no more moles or warts or pimples unless you wish to add some character to your soul. No stinky feet or tough toenails to clip. No fat tummies to whip into shape. No hairy legs to shave.

No smelly underarms. No more plucking of eyebrows or brushing of teeth. No bad breath in death!

WELCOME TO THE AFTERLIFE.

WE HOPE YOU ENJOY YOUR VISIT

FOREVER AND EVER

AND EVER

AND EVER

AND EVER

AND EVER

AND EVER

AND

EVER ...

AND EVER

MORE.

AMEN.

#OneMoreQuestion

"Wow," I say to Samuel.
"This is some brochure!
Plus it's funny.
But I do have one more
important
question."

"Something not
covered?" asks
Samuel.

"Yes. My question
is this:

Does anybody here
ever get

to send messages
to people
down there
on Earth?
Like if it's
really
super crucial?"

Samuel stops gliding.
He puts his hands
on
his hips.
Purses
his lips.

"Girlfriend," he says.
"You want to text
from Heaven?
After what
you went
through? It
killed you."

"It sounds really stupid,
I know. But it's super
important. Something
that will save lives.
If only I can get
the
message
out."

Samuel sighs.

"Some people,"
he says,
"have no
common sense.
You'll just
have to ask
when you get
to your section.
They are the ones
who know
about texting."

I nod. I am trying
to be agreeable
here.

> "What's next?"
> Samuel snorts.
> "You going
> to send
> a selfie
> from Heaven?"

I take a deep breath,
except I guess
there's not
really a need
to breathe,
and then
there's a step
that's not even
a step,

and I just keep

following this
strange angel
Samuel

to my section
of Heaven.

#SoNotHappy

So when
we get there,
I see that
everybody
has a phone
attached
to a wing.
I have wings too!
It's a crazy sight.
All those glossy wings,
with phones
and glowing screens.

I can see
the last
random

text message
every person sent.
There's a lot
of "What's up?"
and "Chill later,"
along with
plain old "Yes,"
"No," "HMU,"
"IDK," and
"OK."

"Wow," I say.
"That's weird.
Why don't I
have a phone?"

"Oh, but you do,"
Samuel says.
"Check under
your left wing."

I do.

And there it is,
that famous
last picture of me
smiling like a banshee.

#HeavenlyCrush

One guy
especially
catches
my eye.

Now
let me try
to explain this
to you.
There can be
crushes in Heaven
too.
It's like
people
are still hot,
but

in an otherworldly
sort of way.

(Hard to explain.)

"What's your name?"
asks the dude.
"Not to be rude,
but you are
super cute."

"Uh … you too," I reply.
"Macy. Macy Elaine Rain."

"Hey, Macy.
John Wayne Worth
was my name on Earth.
Most people here
call me Wayne.
My parents loved
cowboys, obviously."

"I see that."

The guy wears
a cowboy hat.
The brim rims
his green eyes
with black.
He has dimples
and a few little
chin pimples.
(I guess he's
chosen to
add character
to his soul.)

"So
how old
were you
when you
died?" Wayne
asks.

"17."

Those eyes of green

are killing me

                           (if I weren't already

                                      dead).

"Me too!
We have that
in common.
I lived outside
of Seattle,
And my parents
raised cattle.
We had horses,
of course,
and lots of
acres of land.
I played in this
country-punk-
rock-Goth
indie band.
We made the
radio.
One-hit wonders.

They played our song
on all these
stations.
How about you?
Where were you
from?"

I take
a breath,
feel myself lift
like a leaf in the wind.
Having wings
is a little bit
of an
adjustment.

"I'm from Ohio.
Green Line, Ohio.
I died while taking a selfie
and posting it."

Wayne chuckles.

"That sucks."

"It does.
So how about you,
John Wayne Worth?
Tell me everything,
from death back to birth."
(I've become
so much flirtier
than I was on Earth!)

"Well," he says.
"I died while sending a text
to my ex
while riding a motorcycle."
He holds up his wing to show me.

The text says,
"I will never stop loving you."

"Awww," I say.
"That sucks.
Plus, there's love.
That must be tough."

Wayne shrugs.

"Yeah. So, anyway.

I was an only child,

a little bit wild.

Good at heart.

Fairly smart.

My parents

thought the

world turned around me,

their baby boy.

They always said

I gave them joy."

"Awww," I say.

"I was an only child

too. I never knew what

to do with myself when

I was little. I used to wish

for a sister.

Or a brother.

Just somebody other

than just me."

"I agree.
I did that too.
It's like too big of a deal
when you are the only one
for the parents
to love.
Lots of pressure
to be amazing,
you know?"

"Yep. I totally get that."

Our eyes meet,
and I feel a beat
where my heart
used to be.

Celestial connection.
Our conversation is
like a vacation.
Easy. Kicked-back.
Relaxed.

Here are the facts:
I am crushing.
If I had skin,
I'd be blushing.

This John Wayne Worth
is better than any dude
I knew
on Earth.

#JohnWayne

He
Never
Went
To
Spain
Or
To
Maine,
And
It's
Hard
To
Explain,
But
In
My

Heavenly
Brain,
All
I
Can
See
Is

Macy Elaine + John Wayne

My
Whole
Soul
Has
Made
The
Shape
Of
A
Heart.

#MrsWorth

There are weddings
in Heaven!
First comes love.
Then comes marriage.
Then comes Macy
pushing a baby
carriage.
No, wait!
No babies birthed
outside of Earth.
Well then,
all I know
at this moment
is that I keep
seeing
my new name:

Macy Elaine Rain Worth.

Mrs. John Wayne Worth.

Mrs. Worth.

Ms. Macy ER Worth.

MER Worth.

Macy Worth.

This is my rebirth!

#TheSoundsOfHeaven

The Died by Texting
section is hectic.
Constant phone alerts
and sounds all around.
Ringtones:
Midnight Sun and
Space Shuttle and
Starlit
and *Aurora* and *Life's Good*
and *Maple* and *Tropical Fish*.
Notifications:
Crystal and *Dewdrop* and *Ding Dong*
and *Echo*.
Plus *Game Over* and *Pebble* and *Shooting Star*
and *Twinkle*
and *Whistling Bird*.

It's absurd,
all the racket here.
And everybody thinks
Heaven
is *so* peaceful.

#Infinity

You know how
an old-school clock
is just a circle
of numbers with
12 at the top,
6 at the bottom,
ticktock-ticktock
hands moving
forward every
minute?
Well, here
it's all infinity.
No more
minutes.
No more
clocks.

No more
time.
No more
day.
No more
night.
It's just all
about
the light
in the
afterlife.
No more Monday.
No more Tuesday.
No Wednesday or Thursday
or Friday.

No midnight.
No noon.
No April or May
or June.

No more weekends!

No months. No weeks.
No years.
No fear
of being late for a date.
No appointments
to make!

There's nowhere
we have to be
but
here.

#InfinityFlows

Blends together
like a river
that never ends.
Souls
float.
We each
have our own
soul
boat.
Merrily, merrily, merrily, merrily,
Life
Is
But
A
Dream.

Nothing is as
it seems
on Earth.
Nothing is
worth
stressing over.

When you get
here, it's like
you found the
biggest four-leaf
clover ever.

It's like a winning
lottery ticket.

That bucket list
some people make?
About all the places
they want to see
and all the things
they want to do?

They have no clue.

Here in Heaven
you can do and see
everything!

And
it's all for free!
And it's so flippin'
easy! No flat tires
or angry frequent fliers
or engine fires
on trains.
Travel is no longer
a pain!

So, you see,
if only
you knew
what was
coming,
you wouldn't

even need
your dumb old
bucket list.

Because Heaven
is all your wishes
come true!

Nobody is ever bored.

There's so much
to do.
But then again,
if you all knew ...

#Hanging

With
John
Wayne
For
All
Eternity.
And
Best
Of
All

There
Is
No
End ...

#TheForest

So, John Wayne
and I are sitting
in a tree
k-i-s-s-i-n-g.
Not really.
Seriously, though,
there is a forest here.
Green and leafy
and the trees
are like summer *forever*.
They make shade
and shapes
because there's light
and shadows.
The rustle of breeze.
Birds chirp.

And ***John*** Wayne Worth
and I are holding wings!

This is everything
I loved from Earth
and more, because
John Wayne ***Worth***
is here.

A
Squirrel
Is
With
Us
In
The
Forest!
It
Darts
Past
John
Wayne

And
Me,
And
Then
It
Stops
In
Its
Tracks,
Looks
Back,
And
Catches
My
Eye.
That
Squirrel
Knows
I
Am
That Selfie Girl,
And

I
Know
He
Is
That
Squirrel*
From
My
Last
Moments
On
Earth.

* #PlusThatSquirrel

#ThatSelfieGirl2

"Hey! Aren't you
That Selfie Girl?"

You know how they say
you're famous in China?
Well, I'm famous in the sky.

It's a little bit
mortifying,
dying
while taking a picture
of
yourself.

#IWannaHoldYourWing

So
when you hold
wings,
you tell one another
things
that nobody else knows.
I tell John Wayne Worth
about this kid on Earth.
Ryan Dunew.
And his plan
to shoot up
the school.

"Holy crap," he says.
"Snap. We've got to stop it
from happening."

"I know, right?
But how?"

John Wayne tips
back his cowboy
hat and scrunches
up his eyes.
He puts a finger on
his chin, stroking
an imaginary beard.

"This might sound weird,"
he says.
"But we might be able to text."

"From Heaven?"

He nods.
"Yep."

"But who
would we text?"

"His parents.
The school.
Anybody cool
enough to get
the message
and tell
the cops,
ASAP."

"How do we
know people's
numbers?" I ask.

John Wayne laughs.
"Duh, in your contacts,"
he says.
"They don't erase just
because
you happen to be
in Heaven."

He raises his wing,

which raises my wing,
and we both look
at my phone.

"There's that stupid
selfie again. Ugh."

"Yeah, now you have
to look at your face
for all eternity," says
John Wayne. "Not that
it's a bad thing
necessarily."

With the tip of his
wing, John Wayne
pushes my contact's tab,
and they all pop up.

"Just try to call,"
says John Wayne.
"Forget about the text."

So I try Mrs.
Dunew, Ryan's
mom, who helped
organize the
prom.

It rings,
rings, rings,
and then
there's her
voice.

"Hello?"

"Uh, hello," I say.
"It's Macy."

"Hello? Hello?
Is this a telemarketer?
Hello? Hello?"

"It's Macy Rain," I say.

But she hangs up.

"She couldn't hear me,"
I say to John Wayne.

"Bummer. Nothing dumber
than no phone calls
from Heaven.
Try a text."

So I do.
I use the tip
of my wing.

CHECK RYAN'S CLOSET.

HE HAS A PLAN.

SHOOT UP SCHOOL,

END OF MAY.

IT'S MACY RAIN,

AND HE TOLD ME.

 Send.

#NoAnswer

No answer.

        "She must not

        have gotten

        it," I say.

        "No texting from

        Heaven

        to Earth."

        "Well, why didn't

        they tell us that

        at check-in?"

        says John Wayne.

        "What a pain.

        So how's a person

        supposed to communicate?

        We need more information!"

Samuel is walking
past, and he pauses,
swishing his wings.

"We can use things
like rainbows," Samuel says.
"Butterflies, birds, clouds.
They're all allowed.
Oh, and pennies. Many, many
shiny pennies
to be left
all around
down
there."

"But what good
are pennies
and butterflies
and rainbows
and birds
and clouds
without

the words
to go
with them?"
I ask.

Samuel laughs.
"Girlfriend," he says.
"You
tell
me.
It's all a big
mystery."

And so I try
to write words
in fluffy clouds.
I push pennies down
through
holes poked
in the streets,
which is pretty sweet
but not very effective.

I send butterflies
through the horizon,
and birds that chirp.
And I burp
out a rainbow
or two or three.

But it's all unseen.
Not noticed.
Nobody pays attention.
Nobody gets my message.

> "**Ryan Dunew** will still
> shoot up the school,"
> I say to John Wayne.
> "And that's a bunch
> of bull. So. Not. Cool."

#Defeat

John Wayne and
I slump against a tree
in double defeat.
We are beat.

"Serves me right
for being
all about me,"
I say.

"What do you mean?"

John Wayne scoots
closer to me.
Puts his wing
on my knee.

"Well, if only I
hadn't been so
self-centered.
So hell-bent on getting
that selfie
while I was driving.
I wouldn't have ended
up here in Heaven.
And then I would have
made it to the police station
and given them the information.
And Ryan Dunew
would have been *so* busted.
He is not to be trusted!
And I could have changed everything."

"You weren't self-centered,"
says John Wayne.
"You were just being normal.
A normal teenager.
Everybody our age takes—
took—selfies."

"Selfies are selfish.
Egotistic.
Not altruistic.
Greedy, just seeking
praise about your face."

"But," says John Wayne
with an intense gaze.
"You do have a beautiful face.
Who could resist?"

And then the most mystical
thing happens. Better than any
event from Earth.
John Wayne Worth leans close,
and it's the most powerful moment
ever.
We are magnets, attracted
magically:
a strong pull
from him
to me.

*This no longer
feels like
defeat.*

#ThisKiss

John Wayne's lips
lean in, and he
whispers,
> "I want to kiss you.
> Do you?"

> "Want to kiss me?" I ask.
> "No, my lips won't work
> that way."
>> (I always have to be
>> a joker, even
>> at the most
>> smokin' moments.)

> "No," says John Wayne.
> "What I mean is,

do *you*
want to kiss
me?"

I nod. Shy.
I flush. Blush.
I am crushing.
Rushing into
something like
love.

I lean in close
to him.
And the most
electric spark
arcs
between us.

Our lips meet
under that tree,
and this kiss
is a bit of mystic

fairy-tale charm
in that heavenly
place.

Soft, warm, burning,
world-turning.
Like sun meeting sun,
we are joined
as one.

#InfinityKiss

The kiss
lasts for all
eternity.
An infinity
of bliss.
I will miss
his lips
when he
pull away.

This is the
best-ever moment
of my life.
And of my death
too.

I have no clue
what to do
next.

John Wayne
leans away,
tips back his
cowboy hat.

"Wow," he says.
"Pow. Hey, now.
That was like
a bolt.
A jolt
of lightning.
Heart lightning.
Love lightning.
No use fighting
that kind of
lightning.
I'm struck.
You're stuck
with me."

He leans close
once more,
and we begin
the kiss all over
again.

This infinity kiss
is all I'll ever need.
All I'll ever want,
for time without
end.

Amen.

#Forgetting

I'm forgetting all about Ryan Dunew and the school.
I'm forgetting about his guns.

    All
    I
    Need
    Are
    These
    Two
    Suns: John Wayne Worth
                                    And
                                    Me.

    Being away
    from Earth
    is the best place

to be.
But then
Samuel jolts
us both
back to reality.

#BooHiss

"You two crazy kids," Samuel
says. "Kiss, kiss, kiss.
While real problems exist!
Boo, hiss!"

I sigh.
                "Why not be happy?
Things on Earth are crappy.
But we can't change things
anyway."

"She tried.
We tried.
Nobody got
the hints," explains
John Wayne.

"So we may as well
just enjoy
this kiss!"

"Boo, hiss!" says Samuel.
"You two
give up
way too
easy. Not to be cheesy,
but there's
always hope.
Hold on to your
rope. We angels
help people
down there
to
cope."

"But … but …"
I say.
"The *FAQ* brochure
said no more

spying on the people
below. To leave them alone."

"As far as being a creeper,
leave them alone," Samuel says.
"Like, don't check on them
in the shower, spy on their
bathroom breaks, or personal
issues. But when it's a matter of life
and death, heartbeats and breath.
Well then, girlfriend,
we need a divine intervention!"

"So?
What can we do?"
I ask,
and Samuel laughs.

"Stop Ryan Dunew," he says.
"That's what you've got
to do! Save the school.
That dude

needs to get a clue."

"So tell me in plain terms
what to do," I say,
confused.

"We need to
give him good dreams,"
says Samuel.
"Hopes. Goals.
We need to change
his heart
from dark
to light.
We need to fight!
He needs to find
the right
path to follow.
Fill that hollow
spot in
his heart.
Start caring.

And dare
to be a force
of good
in a world
of bad."

John Wayne nods.
"Makes sense," he says.
"You're the boss.
Give us our jobs.
Pronto, dude."

#TheLoftOfDreams

So we follow
Samuel through
a forest to a place
I haven't yet seen.
It's relaxing green
and soothing yellow,
with mellow music
playing soft.

We climb high
to a loft.

> "This is the Dream
> Loft," Samuel says.
> "And the Dream Machine."

He points to a screen.

"Input the name," he says.

I type letters
on the touchscreen:
R-Y-A-N
D-U-N-E-W

The screen flickers,
flutters.

Samuel mutters,
"We'll have dream
access soon. There's
the moon."

A photo
of a full moon
floats across
the screen.

And then the
words

Ryan Dunew's Dreams.
The images
on the screen
grow dark
and scary.

"Very creepy," I
whisper.

"Yes," Samuel says.
"That's why we need
to get into his head.
And his heart.
Start to repair
the damage."

Samuel presses a tab.
"Okay," he says.
"Send light. Bright, bright
light. Close your eyes
if it helps."

I squeeze tight my eyes,

and I'm surprised.
I see light. The light is
shining into
the mind
of Ryan Dunew.

"You know what to do," Samuel says
again and again.
"Get rid of the guns.
Let in the sun.
Become one
with hope
and love.
Allow faith.
Let in the light.
Make the right
choices. Save
yourself.
Save others.
Save your mother.
Save them all."

I open my eyes.

The screen has gone light.

"All right," says Samuel.

"Success! The best ever."

"Are you serious?" I ask.

"Just like that?"

"Just like that," says Samuel.

#TheGodList

A booming voice
fills the air.
     "Macy Elaine Rain," it says.
     "You are next up on the God List."

Samuel's eyes mist.
John Wayne pumps his fist.
     "Yes!" he says.
     "You're next!"

     "What does
that mean?" I ask.
     "What do I do?"

     "There's nothing
to do," says Samuel.

"Except rest.
Be still. God will
soon appear
right over that
hill."

Samuel points.

The brightest light
I've ever seen
makes a sheen
that's almost green.

"Is that God?" I whisper.

Samuel nods.

John Wayne shivers.
"Wow," he whispers.
"I'm getting
goose bumps.
I haven't met God yet."

My eyes are wet.
My heart shudders,
filled with love
so immense.

       "This makes no sense," I say.
        "I am going to meet
        God. This so totally
          rocks!"

        "Being in Heaven
       is like having backstage
       access," Samuel says.
       "It's pretty awesome."

The light hovers
over us, bathes
us in light so bright
that we three
all shine.

The light is love.
Love is the light.

Everything feels right.

We approach the hill.

"Macy Elaine Rain," says God.
"You did a wonderful job.
You stopped
something horrible
from happening
below.
You know
how I feel about that.
I tip my hat
to you, Macy."

That's crazy.
God isn't wearing
a hat.
He doesn't even
have a face.

My heart races.

"Um, thanks," I say.

"And because you,
Macy Elaine, and you,
John Wayne, did something
selfless,
something good,
something amazing,
I will be moving you
from the Died by Texting
section."

"Cool," I say.
"Where to?"

"It's up to you," says God.

"That rocks," says John Wayne.
"I'll go anywhere, as long
as I'm with Macy."

Samuel smacks his forehead.

He rolls his eyes.

"Geez, you two.

Get a room," he says.

"Puppy love."

"Love is love," God replies.

"No matter the age,

it still matters.

It's all that matters."

My heart patters.

"And because

you were

not selfish,

I've taken care

of your families.

Made them

happy," God says.

"I've healed

their grief.

To believe,

just take a look
at the Dream Machine.
Push the key
that says
'Near Future.' "

#OnTheDreamScreen

We go back
to the Dream Machine.
Next thing we see
on the Dream Screen
is a team.
It's Mrs. Dunew and Ryan.
They are buying a cake.
to celebrate.

The guns are gone.
Sold back to a shop.
Ryan has decided to be a cop!

"Congratulations on graduation,"
says Ryan's mom.
"Police academy, here you come!"

And then the screen
changes.
It's the prom.
Ryan's mom
is there,
with flowers
in her hair.
She wears
a long 1920's gown.
It's the *Great Gatsby*
theme,
and there
are all my friends.
Sledge! There's Grandma!
Mom and Dad too.
Dad's wearing a zoot suit.
Mom looks really cute
in a flapper dress …
my flapper dress!

"This is the best!" I say.
"Look, they're smiling."

Dad raises
his phone up high.
He takes a
group selfie.

"Loving life
once again,"
says Samuel.
"That's the goal
for those
left behind
when someone dies.
It all comes
from the light
you shine."

"Nothing to do
with a text,"
John Wayne says.
"Or a call on the phone
to your earthly home."
I start to cry.

"And it's not about
the butterflies," I say.
"It's not about the birds
or the words
in clouds or sending
down pennies.
It's just about
the love.
The love
and the light
and the fight
for those
left behind.
It all starts
in the mind."

"You got that
right," says Samuel.
"Now, girlfriend and her boy,
let's go get
some celebration cake.
Joy!"

#WayLongHome2

We climb
down from
the Dream Loft.
And suddenly
we are in a prom
of our own.
A prom in our
heavenly home!

I am wearing the most
glittery-shimmery gown
of my wildest dreams.
It shines with stars—
real stars—and the hem
is rimmed with edges
of clouds.

"You look downright celestial,"
says John Wayne.

He is all decked out
in a tux
full of the moon
and a bolo tie.
His green eyes
look bright
under a new
cowboy hat.

"Imagine that," says
John Wayne.
"We have a date!"

He produces a
corsage of
white flowers,
and I lift my wing
so he can ring
my wrist with it.

That's when I notice
my cell phone is gone.

"Hey! What happened to
the phone?" I ask.

Samuel laughs.
"It disappears once you're
officially here and no longer
all about yourself," he says.
"Once you're notified by God
that you will be moved
from the Died by Texting
section."

"Cool," says John Wayne.
"Mine is gone too!"

We dance and dance
and laugh and laugh.
"I really like my date,"
says John Wayne.

"That Selfie Girl
is like a pearl
in an oyster.
I'm glad I said
what the heck
and
gave that girl
a whirl."

He twirls me in circles.
"Yeah, that cowboy dude
is pretty cool too," I say.
"I'm glad we get to be
dead together."

"Whatever," says Samuel.
He flicks his wrist.
"You two are too mushy-
gushy for me. And I'm beat.
So I'll leave you
alone
and without your doggone phones!"

Samuel waves goodbye.
I'm so happy I could die.

Oh,
wait.
I'm   already
dead.

Maybe I'm so happy
I could live.

I give John Wayne
another kiss.

This
Is
Bliss.

#TheMusic

And so the music
plays and plays,
and our prom date
goes on and on
like a song.

"Hey!" I say.
"Listen. The song that's
playing is 'Way Long Home.'
I love that song!"

John Wayne
stops dancing.
He pulls away.
Stares at me.

"You know
'Way Long Home'?"
he asks.

I nod.

"Duh," I say.
"It was playing
when I crashed.
When I was taking
the selfie and posting
it, I was saying
how much I loved this
song. It was still playing
as I died.
The whole entire time."

John Wayne shakes his head.
He takes a breath.
"Wow," he says.
"Just. Wow."

"It's by this great band,"

I explain.

"Called Why So Bitter?
I think they're from
the West Coast.
They're the most
amazing band!
You can't understand,
I'm sure,
until you hear them
some more."

John Wayne grins.

"Oh, I've heard them a lot.
They're pretty hot."

"They're amazing!" I say.

John Wayne reaches out.
He strokes my face.

"I used to play
in that band," he says.

"I was the bass player
in Why So Bitter?
Remember, I told
you I played in this
country-punk-rock-Goth indie band
when I was John Wayne
Worth
down on Earth.
Well, that was it.
Why So Bitter?"

"Omigod!" I say.
"I posted it
all over Twitter."

John Wayne
pulls me close.
And we float
to the music.
                "I just knew
                there was
                some connection

that was meant
to be
between you
and me," he says.

"It's magic," I say.
"And not at all
tragic."

"Yeah, but you still
should never
text and
drive,"
he says.
"Not while
you're alive."

"I know, right?"

My heart
is full
of light.

That Selfie Girl
is shining bright.

This is the best night
ever.
Or never.
Whatever.

All I know
is that we are full of glow,

                                                    as the song
                                                    plays on
                                                    forever.

Want to Keep Reading?

Turn the page for a sneak peek at another book from the Gravel Road Verse series: Linda Oatman High's *Teeny Little Grief Machines*.

ISBN: 978-1-62250-883-9

TICKING ... TOCKING

My name is Lexi
        (rhymes with sexy)
McLeen, sixteen,
        and this is what I

believe:

        we are each

Teeny Little
        Grief Machines ...

ticking ...
tocking ...

bombs
programmed to explode ...

if we have not

already

detonated.

MY ENTIRE FAMILY IS A DISEASE

Dad: Alcoholic. Depressive.
Borderline Personality Disorder.

Stepmom: Anorexic. Anger Issues. Bipolar.

The two of them together:
hoarders of cigarettes
and lottery tickets
that never win.

Blaine: Autistic. ADHD.

And me:
artistic.

That's what *they* say
anyway.

I paint
in shades
of blue.

The poetry
is just so

       I

           don't

               explode.

ONCE I CARVED H-A-T-E
ON MY ARM

With scissors.

Just the tip.

Skimming.

Slicing lightly.

A tiny silver nip
of skin.

They thought

I must be a

cutter,

but I wasn't.

There was no knife.

I just
hated
my
life.

It All Started

After we lost
the Baby.

It wasn't our fault.
Carissa,
my little sister,

just died in her white crib
in my bedroom
one night.

Peacefully, in her sleep, all tucked in,
bundled, swaddled, surrounded by pink
princess bumper pads and soft fuzzy blankets.
She wasn't on her stomach.

I can still see her face, sweet,
pink-cheeked,
eyes closed, baby butterflied eyelashes like
tiny splayed paintbrushes wisping her face.
She wasn't breathing. I checked for breath.

Linda Oatman High

Linda Oatman High is an author, a playwright, and a journalist who lives in Lancaster County, Pennsylvania. She holds an MFA in writing from Vermont College and presents writing workshops and assemblies for all ages. In England in 2012, Linda was honored with the *Sunday Times* EFG Short Story Award shortlist. Her books have won many awards and honors, including a Moonbeam Children's Book Gold Medal for *Teeny Little Grief Machines*, in 2014. Information on her work may be found online at www.lindaoatmanhigh.com.